Miss Jump
the Jockey

by ALLAN AHLBERG

with pictures by
ANDRÉ AMSTUTZ

PUFFIN

PUFFIN BOOKS

Published by the Penguin Group
Penguin Books Ltd, 80 Strand, London WC2R 0RL, England
Penguin Group (USA), Inc., 375 Hudson Street, New York, New York 10014, USA
Penguin Books Australia Ltd, 250 Camberwell Road, Camberwell, Victoria 3124, Australia
Penguin Books Canada Ltd, 10 Alcorn Avenue, Toronto, Ontario, Canada M4V 3B2
Penguin Books India (P) Ltd, 11 Community Centre, Panchsheel Park, New Delhi – 110 017, India
Penguin Group (NZ), cnr Airborne and Rosedale Roads, Albany, Auckland 1310, New Zealand
Penguin Books (South Africa) (Pty) Ltd, 24 Sturdee Avenue, Rosebank 2196, South Africa

Penguin Books Ltd, Registered Offices: 80 Strand, London WC2R 0RL, England

puffinbooks.com

First published by Viking 1980
Published in Puffin Books 1980
035 - 35

Text copyright © Allan Ahlberg, 1980
Illustrations copyright © André Amstutz, 1980
All rights reserved

Educational Advisory Editor: Brian Thompson

Set in Century Schoolbook by Filmtype Services Limited, Scarborough
Manufactured in China

British Library Cataloguing in Publication Data
A CIP catalogue record for this book is available from the British Library

ISBN: 978-0-14031-241-6

Mr Jump was a jockey.
He rode in races.
He won silver cups, gold plates
and lots of money.
Mrs Jump was a jockey too.
So was Master Jump.
His name was Jimmy.

Uncle Jump was a jockey.

Grandma Jump was a jockey.

Miss Jump was *nearly* a jockey.

Miss Jump's name was Josie.
Every birthday she said,
"Am I old enough to be a jockey yet?"
And Mr and Mrs Jump said, "Nearly!"
Every Christmas she said,
"Am I old enough yet?"
And they said, "Not long now!"

One Christmas Josie Jump
was sitting up in bed.
She was opening her presents.
There was a jockey's hat
and a jockey's shirt.
There were jockey's trousers
and jockey's boots.
There was a talking doll,
a train set,
an apple, an orange,
a bag of sweets,
– and a *horse*!

Josie Jump jumped out of the window,
jumped on the horse,
and galloped round to her parents' room.
"Am I a jockey now?" she said.
"Yes," said Mr Jump.
Josie Jump fell off her horse.
". . . and no," Mrs Jump said.

After Christmas Josie Jump went
everywhere with her horse.
She went to her friend's house
with him.
She went to the shops
with him.

She went to *school*
with him!

Josie also went to the races with him.
But she did not ride in the races.
The horse was too young.

When his birthday came, Josie Jump said,
"Is he old enough to ride in the races yet?"
And Mr and Mrs Jump said, "Nearly!"

When his next birthday came she said,
"Is he old enough yet?"
And they said, "Not long now!"

BLOW!

A few days later
Mr Jump hit his thumb
with a hammer.
"Now I cannot ride in
the big race!" he said.

Mrs Jump dropped a horse-shoe on her toe.

OUCH!

OUCH!

Jimmy Jump got a splinter in his bottom. "Now we cannot ride in the big race!" they said.

Uncle Jump was on his holidays.

Having a lovely time

Grandma Jump's horse had a sore throat.

The next morning Josie Jump
jumped out of the window,
jumped on her horse
and galloped round to her parents' room.
"Can I ride in the big race?" she said.
"Yes," said Mr Jump.
Josie galloped round and round the house.
"The sooner the better," Mrs Jump said.

Now it was the day of the big race.
Josie Jump lined up with the other riders.
Her family were in the crowd.
The King and Queen were in
the royal box.

The race began.
The crowd cheered, "Hooray, hooray!"
"They're off!"
Josie Jump came to the first fence
– and jumped it.
"Come on, Josie!"
shouted Mr and Mrs Jump.

Josie came to the second fence
– and jumped that.
"Keep going, Josie!"
Jimmy Jump shouted.

Josie came to the third fence
– and fell off!
"Don't stop, Josie!"
shouted Grandma Jump.

Josie Jump jumped up,
jumped on her horse
and kept going.
She jumped the next fence,
and the next.
She jumped four more fences.
She jumped the last fence
– and was the winner!

The crowd cheered, "Hooray, hooray!"
"The winner!"
The King and Queen cheered too.

The King shook hands with Josie Jump.
He gave her a gold cup
and lots of money.
Josie Jump said,
"Am I as rich as the Queen now?"
And the King said, "Nearly!"

Josie Jump went home with her family.
She put the money in her money-box.
She put her horse to bed.
She went to bed herself . . .
and slept till morning.

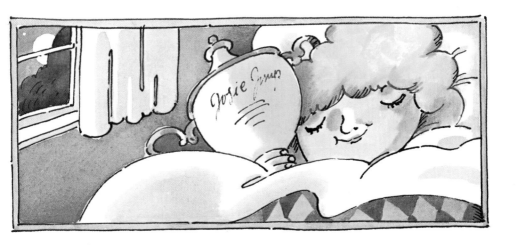

The End